Moonglade

David Edgar Grinnell

Curious Corvid
PUBLISHING

To My Muse: Megan Kibler

Preface

Moonglade is a mausoleum which houses not only the ghosts of past lovers, but past versions of the self. Percy Bysshe Shelley once wrote, "A poem is the very image of life expressed in its eternal truth." This is the essence of what poetry is to me as a writer. Poetry is such an intimate form of writing and expression that every poem in this collection depicts remnants of who I was and am. This is vulnerability at its finest, which I grant to anyone who takes the time to read these poems. Writing this collection over the years was the scariest, and yet most cathartic experience. It made me confront my inner self. It made me see the toxic faults and patterns in myself that I never wanted to admit existed. The themes of love, loss, despair, and hope are all present in this collection's context.

This collection was initially written 2018 to 2020 but has now been expanded to include pieces from the following two years. The first version was published inde-pendently as *Phases of Love's Moon* and contained sixty poems. This second version, renamed *Moonglade,* includes an additional forty poems. These one-hundred poems acknowledge William Shakespeare, whose work first in-spired me to become a poet, and influences my poetic style — though this collection expands beyond the Shakespear-ean influence. There were more transformations I needed to express as an "image of life in its eternal truth." Trans-formation, like in *Ashes,* is a difficult process. There were times where I explored the darkest depths of my mind, and I didn't know if I would make it out alive. My hope for anyone who finds this work is that they discover their own voice. In every sentiment and truth of my experience, I hope you find a catharsis; because many voices like mine and others are silenced. Pain, gloom, and sorrow are so real that sometimes there is no energy to do anything for hours, days, months, or years. I can't express enough how important mental health is. Yet — it's an area of health that does not get the care or compassion it needs. Many stay silent and suffer internally because of fear of rejection and the walls that they build for themselves. It is because depression is a scary thing to openly talk about from such a burden. Many are alone because of not only depression, but because people grieve in pain differently.

In some ways, this work is very painful for me. Letting go of these pieces that have been a part of me for so long is a necessary part of self-growth, but it isn't easy. These poems are a snapshot of life — both the emotions they depict, and the moments in which they were written. As I reflect on these poems, I also see growth and transformation. This is why the title *Moonglade* — meaning the bright reflection of moonlight on a body of water is the central theme of this work. The title also represents the various phases of the moon; how they reflect, mirror, and correlate with the self. The order of the poems is chronological, showing the various phases of what I once was, and what I still struggle with. Each poem portrays the endless cycles; stages of love, self-love, and relationships. In the words of Lord Byron, "The great object of life is sensation — to feel that we exist, even though in pain."

May you experience such sensations of existence in these poems.

-    David Edgar Grinnell

  February 2022

Introduction

True love finds a way to crawl out of the commercial carcass of the modern corporate world in order to reclaim its rightful place, and continue seeping through the veins of the vulnerable, as it always has. Occasionally, a writer comes along willing to ignite a flame that expedites this condition.

David Grinnell is one of the sincerest individuals I have known, and his authenticity is an ever-present component of his poetry. My time studying alongside him under professors that have inspired us has provided me with unique insight into his writing style; the details of which may help a curious reader look at his work through a different lens. The truth expressed has spoken for itself as his personal growth coincided with that of the collection. This imbues his writing with a pure blend of real-to-life highs and lows that resemble the gradual change Grinnell made while becoming an author capable of tapping into both a wide spectrum of experiences (exemplified in poems such as "Tarot of Ashes") and a relatability (exemplified in poems such as "My Parents") that is able to transmit those messages to any interested reader willing to dig deeply enough to find the hidden puzzles in the form of acrostics weaved into his literature.

When reading Grinnell's poetry, relatability pours through. I believe he is able to grant his literature this essence through his mastery of vulnerability. Confidence is an important trait to see in one's self, especially when in the search of love, however, at some point in this journey of two people, they must reveal their true selves.

In order to dedicate one's true self to the other, a person has to reveal insecurities; a difficult but necessary part of an honest, trust-based relationship. Grinnell is able to depict individuals in realistic, impactful ways by showing their individual struggles, their mutual challenges, and the resulting conditions they face due to both their actions and the predicaments of fate.

It would be unfair to have a reader go further without an understanding of the time in which this text was written. *Moonglade* has become both the product and re-flection of the time that produced it. For this reason, Grinnell speaks for more than just himself through this text as it brings forth the strife of this historical time. It is the voice of the resilience of the common man's way of life in a time of cosmic horror. Let this be a note to ponder while enjoying this collection and remember to take caution when approaching the tale that has taken many great minds on the quest of creativity that often leads to an early demise.

I am not being modest in saying Grinnell knows a great deal more about poetic structure than myself. Throughout his work, one will find countless different verse forms taken from a diverse range of cultural backgrounds and literary traditions. The same goes for the syntax and grammar within his writing. Poetry and modern art alike have taken many obscure and groundbreaking forms across the ages; however, I argue that Grinnell using a more traditional assortment of styles is much more appropriate for the subject matter, as a great deal of love's charm lies in the foundations of social constructs, or the "dance," so to speak, that takes place alongside these emotions. This is echoed by a beautiful analogy in the poem "Red Wine," however, its comparison of wine to love could be taken further to reflect how good authentic wines must be held dearly and cherished much like romantic traditions such as courtship and commitment.

For this reason, tradition, nostalgia, chivalry, and emotion are all able to transcend the monetized interpretations of what love should look like in the eyes of the modern world and convey authenticity that takes us back to reading about love in Greek, Roman, Norse, and Shakespearean plays. Romance is not without challenges. This can be seen clearly in the last lines of "Melancholy." This collection makes the reader ponder what their first love felt like, before expectations and memories were able to cloud anticipation.

Grinnell has definitely spent parts of his life being quite a savvy traveler, as well. Due to his knowledge of an assortment of cultural backgrounds, his literature is lightly seasoned with an array of various references to other languages, culinary practices, and travel destinations. If those are of interest to you, an open eye may bring them to your attention.

Grammar, etymology, and syntax: let's jump right in! As poetry is an artform with deep traditional roots, it is only fitting when discussing a long-standing cultural construct to utilize the language of the era in which it grew. For this reason, especially in the earlier poems in the collection, words like "thy," "thee," and "thine" are used. This archaic verbiage is even more prevalent in "Dear Grace." This is especially interesting to examine in the poem "The Breakup" where the usage of "you" shifts to the usage of "thee." In modern day, the usage of "you" is more common, however, in Early-Modern English, it was a more intimate way to address the subject. This shift reinforces the transition of affection away from the subject within the poem.

The use of Latin, Greek, Welsh, and German are present as well. If you are not a linguist, do not run for the hills just yet: there are footnotes. The poem titled "Regenzeit" translates to "Rainy Season" from German, for example. The final couplet of the poem leaves a powerful impactful impression before and after translation.

Writers and poets alike often find their love of poetry more strongly aligned with a specific verse form the way that music aficionados often have preferences towards specific genres. Grinnell tackles a wide array of forms throughout this work, so readers are sure to find poems that resonate with them personally. If you are familiar with the common Spenserian Stanzas, Shakespearean Sonnets, Lord Byron's favorite Ottava Rima, Haikus, Limericks, and Blank Verse forms, you will be sure to find pieces that are familiar to you.

Grinnell also strays from these forms in some poems or finds variations of these forms that suit his artistic direction. Curtal Sonnets and Envelope Sonnets are examples of derivatives. While meter is one example of innovating within these mediums, readers should grant equal attention to rhyme. While some poems within the collection such as "Affection" do a great deal to fit rhyme patterns, others such as "Grief" stray from these patterns. "Forgiveness" is a good example of a poem written in the "Rispetto" style, while "Affection" is written in a similar form with various liberties taken with rhyme patterns. "Candlelight" is perhaps the most ambitious verse form tackled, aside from the masterpiece that is "Confliction."

Poetic structure is truly at the heart of this work. This can be seen in the various poems directly named after the forms they embody. "Blood Quill" is named for the Blood Quill form, "Nocturne" is written in the Nocturna musical/poetic form, "Raven Sonata" is named for the Raven Fly form, and "Candlelight" which is of course written in the Candlelight verse form.

Now onto the poem structures that I lack the authority to comment upon. Rhyme Royal was used and popularized by Chaucer much like Ottava Rima was used and popularized by Byron. The Sestain, Triolet, and Forlorn Suicide forms can also be spotted within the collection. The Sestain form can be identified by its ABABCC rhyme format and iambic pentameter. The poem "Bioluminescence," meaning "living light," was written as a Triolet: an eight-line poem with an interesting rhyme structure of its own. A desire to write in Forlorn Suicide format is typically met with a blueprint for a UFO and a prescription for Prozac, its rarity and complexity are such that a guide to its understanding is too large a task for a humble page like this one. All these forms do a good job of bringing a variety of shades to a subject that will put you through a diverse range of emotions, and they are all interesting to study in their own right.

The latter parts of the collection are home to a set of poems that follow a relationship from start to finish, bringing in the analogy of the phases of the moon to accompany the various stages of a relationship. The first of the collection is an introduction, fittingly called "Phases of Love's Moon." The new moon phase is represented by "Attraction," the waxing crescent by "Harbor Perk." A cafe in Ashtabula, Ohio the first quarter is represented by "The Choice," while "Gibbous Heart" is more directly named in reference to the waxing gibbous stage. "Storm Moon" represents the full moon. The name, "Storm

Moon," is a reference to a specific full moon in February that is also occasionally called the "Death Moon" or "Quickening Moon" in spiritual cultures. The waning gibbous is represented by the poem "Dissemination." "Forgiveness," the Rispetto form referenced earlier, is representative of the last quarter, and the waning crescent, the last stage of the moon cycle, ties up the cycle in "The Surrender."

Grinnell's writing is in many ways paying homage to a lost art. In an age of emotional and physical isolation, (an overall sub-par time to be alive, let alone in love) Grinnell reminds us what is at the core of true emotion. He reflects on and portrays love alongside hope, melancholy, and even occasional despair. Although his work is certainly contemplative, his short poems are also simultaneously perfectly proportioned for meditation and literary analysis alike. Enjoy a rare treat in a confusing dark world, and perhaps find inspiration to piece together some hope and joy in trying times.

-    Tsezariy Patrick Iablonski

Heart to Heart

You rest your head and snuggle on my chest.

Amongst the blades of grass and gentle care

The scent of your long hair puts me at rest,

For what matters is this moment we share

Time wains; nothing ever lasts forever.

Do not worry, the future that awaits,

Enjoy what we have right now together

Listen, your heart will always have a place.

The warmth of the sun's rays fades a distance

The courtyard's water plays a softened tune;

Your body gives warmth to my existence.

As our souls intertwine between love blooms,

My eyes grow heavy and begin to close

You, my love, are the blanket of my woes.

Forbidden

The image of her beauty stains my eyes

As her short dark hair meanders in flight,

Oh thine, deep brown eyes, listen to my cries,

Thy soft warm lips beckon my soul with might

The echoes of thy voice set me alight,

But my mind and hands are forced in wastage,

The red in thy cheek and scarf tempts my sight

My heart's blood seeps to know thine own bondage,

Helpless am I, the woman who holds me hostage.

Red Wine

Shall love itself be compared to red wine?

The bottle shape glass conceals its beauty

Lovers twist the corkscrew, ready to dine?

Let it breathe or pour for the gomuti [1]

Its scent alludes to my affectedness,

We have swirled this relationship before

Its taste savors of my addictiveness,

The year of our vintage urges me more

Why call for the open bottle we had?

I left us to sour, haunted am I

Pick me up, take a swig, how is this bad?

Our taste rotten ruins us high and dry

As this hangover is knowingly wrong,

I cannot help but sing us the same song.

---

[1] Gomuti – A sweet Malaysian sap used in wine.

Dear Grace,

Drown thy sorrow

For thou hatest me and I hate thee.

Thine eyes displease the sun's morrow

Thou sobs for fun and its music please't me.

Thou art shrewest Grace;

Shag from man to man

Even Satan shuns thy face,

Get thee hence, find another plan.

If thou ever thinketh of me,

Know thou art the greatest burden

As thou art meant to be;

Crawl thy grave, receive thine guerdon. [2]

The angels and demons shall not care

Even the Lord will not heed thy prayer.

----

[2] Guerdon – Reward or payment.

The Breakup

After the New Year is a beginning
That love once there is not in your own bed,
The touch of her waist in your arms stinging
As the scent of her hair looms in your head,
The words said shatter the heart once living
Now the emptiness consumes our souls dead,
I love you, but we cannot truly be
Forgive me, and release me to be free.

Please don't mistake the love I carried thee
For our love was beautiful and sincere,
The limits of me have been drowned at sea
Misery strikes my subconsciousness clear
As our relationship sinks from the quay
You my love don't take the role of emir, [3]
My heart is breaking, I have tried to say
"Take independence; if not, I can't stay."

---

[3] Emir – An independent ruler.

My Valentine

I declare, "Will you be my Valentine?"

Shakespeare and Chaucer romanticize it

But do you, my Valentine, know its twine?

Yes, Saint Valentine died, his loving wit

However, there is a darker tidbit,

The feast of Lupercalia was sane

As men sacrificed a goat, dog, and hit,

Then whipped the women with the hides just slain,

Young women lined up; swat them fertile match-
make-chain.

Beloved Poet

The clouds in the sky churn dark and are gray

As thoughts of you linger all through my mind,

Your picture on the screen glows, my hope's ray

Tell me my words did not frighten you blind

Show me the words that not lead us astray,

Write lover poet, why aren't you online?

It's been a few days since we last conversed

I will make this poem's next stanza well-versed.

OkCupid is not the greatest site

But you my poet are a special gem,

I smile when my phone chimes in your light

My heart aches to your imaged diadem, [4]

The language of your text lights my stars bright,

You are a diamond and nothing like them

You're a woman, staring into fire;

I pray my worth will never expire.

---

[4] Diadem – A tiara-like headdress that signifies sovereignty.

Rejection

Step outside, what do I knowingly see?

White crystal snow shimmering from God's gaze

With a prayer, my hope's ray did not agree,

My worth has expired, gone is my chaise [5]

Gone is my heart which was set in a blaze

By you, my lover poet, ashes seep,

My fragmented soul tormented dismays

And all that remains are the shards cut deep,

"Romantically, it's not there." Texts she as I weep.

------

[5] Chaise – A carriage consisting of two wheels and calash top: drawn by a single horse.

Affection

My heart aches with every tender sweet kiss,
The touch of your embrace tugs my heart's strings
As the blue in your eyes is heaven's bliss,
My soul now, forever, and ever sings.

No sonnet can suffice my love to you
None of these words are enough to express
And no song written; performed can be true,
To show that my love will never subdue.

Grief

It's Sad when you know she doesn't love you,
You rethink the times you once had thought true
"I need a break" said she as your heart bleeds
Your soul in limbo wanders restlessly
The mind doubts, wondering what went wrong seeds,
Then the time flies as you lie there and die,
The love once there changes to grief; you cry
Agony to fill the space in your room
But silence is your only loyal friend
The sun sets, darkness embodies your tomb,
She ghosts, and will haunt you forevermore
As you build walls within your crypt to mend,
In my casket I wait for another
Open, fair lady; not like the other.

Venom

The day is cold, and the clouds are my mask,

As the siren's coffee touches my lips [6]

The scars of your kisses mend in my cask

Alone, I wait as your image seen thrips,

You and your friend stain my sight more than Slask [7]

Leave, I do not need your sob-petty scripts

Once my lover, now embodies to thresh

The serpent whose fangs masticate my flesh.

---

[6] Starbucks Coffee logo is a siren.
[7] Slask – A region between Poland rich in coal and iron ore.

Obsidian Wings

White wings contorted never touch the sky

As my wings once loved, held, and shielded her

Blood seeps from my blinded eyes, not known' why

The love she once gave me I still prefer;

Her dagger is my darkness gloom succor [8]

Wine cannot numb the poison of her blade;

The feathers strew black I watch them abrade. [9]

---

[8] Succor – Assistance in difficult times.
[9] Abrade – wear away.

Shayla

She was the first in the room with beauty

Heaven's bliss was the blue inside her eyes,

As the months pass on, her heart withered sooty [10]

Yearning for the love she once gave me dies

Longing for the solace of her embrace

Always, is the memory of her face.

---

[10] Sooty – The blackest black.

Cadaverous

The winter is cold and barren in white

As is my heart haunted by lovers' past,

Ghost of Christmas old, I knew five years' night

Your shadow looms every memory cast

While ghost of Christmas present towers vast,

Oh, spirit yet to come, where is your scythe?

Wrap me in your cloak for a love most lithe. [11]

---

[11] Lithe – Graceful movement; bending with ease.

Suicide

Fall into Darkness

What is evil incarnate?

Depression distrait.

Bioluminescence

The girl of my childhood meanders bright,

Memories flash, a love most innocent

Sparks ignite, her image seen in the light

The girl of my childhood meanders bright,

Twenty years have gone, the woman I write

Revives my heart bioluminescent

The girl of my childhood meanders bright,

Memories flash, a love most innocent.

Pretext

She likes me, she likes me not

Reply already

Did our kiss mean nothing naught?

My childhood neddy! [12]

You can text me anytime now…

I double texted

New Year's Eve plan disavow?

This is pretexted!

---

[12] Neddy – Speaker refences childhood friend as an "ass…"

Resolution

Cheers, long live the New Year 2020

Refine a modern-day age of flappers,

At a house bar surrounded by my friends

"Love her endless" says my suit, an Eve penny

Apple snags my view; cultivate dappers [13]

Ubiquitous her beauty as contends,

Racket my soul, she is my Impaler,

Erode my heart of stone midnight clappers

Noisily your sounds echo, my past transcends,

A new hope from online, will she tailor?

Now cleanse.

---

[13] Dappers – Neat and trim men in dress and appearance.

3 A.M.

Oh, Tinder is the night!

This woman I know alright

How tempting to know

Will she be in sough?

Oh, Tinder, I swiped right!

Freitag

Freitag-Freitag [14]

Give a tug heart,

Polly-drug me

A hug, new love.

[14] German for Friday.

Dear Friend,

Tinder you were, Tinder you are not,

A woman you like, chase her you aught,

Hopeless romantic,

Never be frantic;

I am only a friend to be sought.

Lauren

Look into those eyes, beautiful deep brown

Awakens my hope, she is the tailor

Ubiquitous her beauty, all slows down

Romantic music plays; the heart frailer,

Earnest the desire opens the soul

Nimble my eyes, I wait; never you shoal.

Affinity

A change; shoal I thought she was my tailor

Communication ceased, no attraction

Disappointment, she is now my vailer [15]

Shroud my eyes, darkness descends a fraction

Who will be brave and unveil the wailer?

A voice, new, yet familiar calls action

I am released from this petrifaction,

Will she be another movie trailer?

---

[15] Vailer – one who vails. (Obsolete.)

Unrequited Love

Chivalry is a woman's prized gemstone

Am I the Jorah to your Daenerys? [16]

I admire you from afar, your throne

Of power is the Welsh meaning *Cerys,* [17]

Zeal burns fierce as my soul withers Ceres, [18]

Urbane is my heart in vain, your beauty [19]

Zhooshes your academics, my duty [20]

Abides if I'm chivalrously knighted,

Near your side I'd be your Queensguard sooty

Next to you, I tremble; Greyscale benighted

An unrequited love only cited.

---

[16] Jorah, Daenerys, Greyscale – Read *A Game of Thrones.*
[17] Cerys – Welsh for love.
[18] Ceres – Roman goddess of agriculture and fertility.
[19] Urbane – Notably Polite.
[20] Zhoosh – Make more exciting, lively, or attractive.

Algid Queene

Is she too self-absorbed in her own work?

Her wit is lit, but how is my spirit?

Unrequited love fell in a cirque

Walls are high, fantasy, I'm a pierrot [21]

A fool doomed, a fool doomed in dispirit

My mind banished in this valley broken

The heart crystalizes, cold, who will inspirit?

"Winter is coming," what does this foretoken?

The most beautiful woman; nobody woken.

---

[21] A male performer dressed in white with a whitened face from French pantomime traditions.

Melancholy

I cannot abuse the chivalric code,

A woman is not a sexual object

As my heart atrophies with every goad [22]

To get my everlasting soul beat wrecked

'Tis an endless cycle, the moon deflect

Relationship after relationship,

Love after love; my hope dies with courtship.

---

[22] Goad – Give heart or courage to.

Midnight

Tinder, a picture

Match, a new glimmer of hope

Message, exchange text.

Megan

Music is her passion as my passion,

Effervescence consumes my soul's desire [23]

Golden blonde hair, pure blue eyes, no dispassion

Attains me like no other lit fire,

Nightingale sings, I forsaken all shown,

The undying flame of the Nightingale

Scorches the chambers of my heart once known

Sings, shines; burns brighter than a fighting sail

To be her lover muse, her sky of stars,

She is the spirit to my bloodstone tune [24]

Can't immortalize her with my guitars,

Love is only the phases of the moon

My Nightingale, your beauty forever;

Shakespeare's muse can't withstand this endeavor.

---

[23] Effervescence – Sparkle.
[24] Bloodstone – Spiritual stone to overcome any distress.

Regenzeit

Out there, somewhere, I will meet you someday

Until that day comes, I will wait for you

To come into my life; into your heart

With mine; the days we have, never we fade,

Your picture makes my heart soar with delight

My hopes high, let these devout words assure

Ich steh' im regen und warte auf dich,

Ich warte im regen und steh' für dich. [25]

---

[25] Regenzeit – rainy season in German.
"I stand in the rain and wait on you.
I wait in the rain and stand for you."

Phases of Love's Moon

Starry Night, how the moon reflects the light,

The water shimmers, the stars above gleam

The sky clear, across me, a beautiful view,

No rose or lily for love will suffice

On how they snuggle, I long for your embrace

Let us build our boat, cuddle till the dawn

Face every storm and phase of love's moon,

Our eyes lock, caress, every tender kiss.

Attraction

The new moon is a wonderfully pure phase
As the heart blooms, the temptation conceives
Love to blind all reason, the flower braze
Blackens whole if the growth rapidly weaves
The hopeless romantic I am don't craze
Take love easy, slow, and admire her leaves
Because her petals have a unique tinge
I am in no rush; flirt, but do not singe.

Harbor Perk

The waxing crescent is the foundation

Where a relationship is like a ship,

It takes two to build communication

Two to grow together prepare the trip

Using honesty, trust. The compass tip

Binds us, the look in your eyes, you take me

Like no other has; see what my eyes see?

The Choice

First quarter moon how wondrous you are

Half illuminated, half shadowed, choose

My fate in her hands, my heart in her grasp

My soul weighs her judgment, am I worthy?

Worthy of her love, worthy to be hers?

I stand, wait, mind daunt; the phone screen still black

Vibrates none time abates phone light and texts

Busy she is, this I know, hope remains

My words obvious mean not to rush you,

I like you, gentle, respectful, text soon.

Gibbous Heart

Take a leap of faith, reckless behavior

Waxing gibbous I cannot blame it now…

My honesty, the filter in my head

Hurts me, what will be our growing bond?

Sing "Friends, Lovers or Nothing" what is gained? [26]

Nothing else, I wish to be your lover

You wound me, I myself, emotions cover.

---

[26] Listen to "Friends, Lovers or Nothing" by John Mayer.

Storm Moon

Full moon, the peak, the buzz, its crescendo

Nightingale lights up; the dream time landscape,

You know me more than what I know of you

Sing the reckoning, or moment of truth,

I wait for your cue; your own clarity

Shall I write comedy or tragedy?

What is the realization of your desire

For us; our own little musical play?

Dissemination

"I do want to say that I do like you."

The light gradually decreasing, smaller,

Waning gibbous her words disseminate

The fiber of my internal being

The light gradually decreasing, smaller,

Out bad habits, stresses, negative thoughts

The fiber of my internal being

Reflects these words: "I'm concerned about time."

Out bad habits, stresses, negative thoughts

Waning gibbous her words disseminate

Reflects these words: "I'm concerned about time."

"I do want to say that I do like you."

Forgiveness

Last quarter moon I must find forgiveness
For the day and hour draws near, beat drum,
Nightingale, my heart bleeds impulsiveness
As my mind numbs, knowing what is to come.

Your text soliloquy the final act
Will hurt, break me bloody as you redact
These woeful walls shall burn my insides slow
I must have forgiveness to let this go…

The Surrender

What is done is done

Waning crescent surrender;

My Nightingale flies.

What is gone is gone

The light is withering spent,

Haunted; *End of Play*?

Dave the Brave?

Jenna Baker, will you be my maker?

I'm not proposing; I am no faker

Just don't send me to the undertaker.

Dave the brave was already in his grave

Elegies read, prayers said, flowers dead wave

His unwritten obituary, knave!

Ding-dong ditch, did the bells ring spring has sprung?

I was flung, I was strung, and even hung

Or was I just another piece of dung?

Blood Quill

March thirteen, the blood quill

Scrawled her to my nature

Springs "are we going to make this a thing?"

Her answer echoes still

Our Facebook portraiture

Is the reminder of our wellspring.

March thirteen, the red ink

Bled through her name run dry,

And its scent never lets me forget

The love we had did sync

Do you think now to try?

Different we are, anew, no regret.

Confliction

Keep me in your thoughts

As days pass; no contact

To save me from the shadows

Hope fades; where is her tact?

Ache stomach in knots

Rot forlorn heart [27]

Ill my soul trots

No message to extract

Ember; candle of woes.

Only she can attract

Pull me from these spots

Beautiful art;

Loneliness

Rips me apart

Darkness only dots

The walls to cave abstract;

---

[27] The poem format is called "Forlorn Suicide."

Vines seep into my skull grows

Thorns to mend and distract

The mind from gunshots.

Where do I start?

Sleeplessness

Kills me

Hopelessness

Cannot depart;

She's not an ersatz [28]

I must remain intact

For I can see the meadows.

Bilateral contract

I know your own nots

Take heart; impart

Openness

And see

Love.

---

[28] Ersatz – Artificial or inferior substitute.

Nocturne

It was her and I in the country night,

The brisk cold composes a dreamy air

My car blackest-black glistens in moonlight,

"Look how it sparkles" said her voice with grace

The stars clear, her across from me, I stare

And feel the solace of her warm embrace,

My glasses fog, steam, as her figure leans

Kisses my cheek with the most tender care;

I hug, kiss her cheek, melody serene.

Raven Sonata

The raven dreams and lets me fly
Her beauty vivid, stands, sings
Crowds gather; me next to her, nigh,
Play my six-string guitar rings.

The raven dreams as I hold her
And feel her hourglass waist,
"You two together?" They confer,
Arms gentle, her smile graced.

The raven dreams, I desire more sends
"No, we are on the borderline of friends."

Prelude Plague

My dearest most cherished one do not fret

Of this fate that consumes and torments all

You are not alone, we are a duet.

Far we are, isolated, just a call

Away; I'm still here to sooth all your fears

As the coronavirus spreads to sprawl.

Remember; think of me, and wipe those tears

This disease orchestrates the prelude plague

But this heart beats the music of the spheres.

Time, space, and distance will drain us both vague

As all around shuts down; state borders close

I won't be able to drive to you Meg.

No matter how separate we are I've chose

My dearest most cherished one to enclose.

Dissonance

There is so much dread, I'd rather be dead,

Now withdrawn in complete isolation

How do I get rid of this sensation?

There is nothing I can do in her stead.

If I were dead, who would miss me then?

Not you, Meg none know of my mentation [29]

The demons in my head, write weeping pen.

[29] Mentation – Thoughts.

Candlelight

Kindled flame embers,

Envy remembers

Love that was once there,

Sustenance bare;

Emptiness take

Your heartache;

Wind howls

Wax melts

Hardens

Slow,

Fade,

Sleep,

Cold,

Love;

See

My

Candlelight wasting away?

Chain of Abolition

Memories pour
As I think of you
The wedding where we met,
The first date you held my hand;

Our first hug
At your front door;
My heart from then knew
That we were a rare set
And our second date was grand;

Met mom,
Your house snug
Your dad's jokes roar
As smiles flew
In your room won't forget
The talks, the first kiss, our strand.

Us

In palm

Held and tug

Made love and more

Emotions, pure, true,

Our time spent, no regret

The memories flash; disband.

Timorous

Should I be worried, the silence that falls?

No texts chime, reread the messages sent

Nothing is this a reason to lament?

Minutes, hours, and days form barrier walls

Rescue me from my attic high above

With the words, emojis, and length written;

Am I not the man with whom you're smitten?

Save me from my doubts; text her, mourning dove.

Envelope draft, should these words disappear? [30]

If not, will she still think of me the same?

I do not want this connection to end

Nor lose what we have made to be endear

Will chance be a worthy or an ill name?

How long should I wait for her reply send?

---

[30] The use of the word "envelope" brings attention to the envelope sonnet form being used here.

The Train [31]

Are we just strangers caught in the same web of
dreams,

Falling through the same pages,

Gripping on at the same seams?

Or a gunner in the trenches;

Fighting in the crossfire between them and us,

And you're not giving up

Until you catch the train back home,

A hero.

But I'm safe in silence,

Out of my mind with you in mind,

And imagination won't suffice

Or quiet the beating of my heart

---

[31] This poem was written by Rachel Habraken for David Grin-
nell and gifted him with permission to make it part of this col-
lection. Appreciation goes out to the poet of this piece.

I wish you were here.

If peace found my mind would you have me
Fight my own battles?
Well I know I could stay strong.

If I'm safe in silence,
Out of my mind with you in mind,
And imagination won't suffice
Or quiet the beating of my heart
I wish you were here.

If only you could stay and never go
But the battles keep calling you out,
So onwards you always go.

But I'm safe in silence,
Out of my mind with you in mind,
And imagination won't suffice
Or quiet the beating of my heart
I wish you were here.

I'll wait here, wishing

Until you catch the train back home,

My hero.

Coloratura Coda

"You'll Never Walk Alone" rings in my head [32]

Hearing you sing it as I lie in bed,

Your voice reminds me I'm never alone

A gentle feeling aches within my core,

You comfort me like nobody before.

I close my eyes, headphones, your melody

Plucks my heartstrings its tender remedy

Caress; blankets me its lullaby tone,

As my soul intertwines to every sound

Your warm image residing in is found.

I want you to be the first and last thing

I see, hear, hold to my remaining days

On this earth as I drift off to sleep stays

Forever, my love, a place where you sing.

---

[32] Song title from the musical play "Carousel."

Luscinia

Lachrymose is the chair I sit
Unconsciously it does emit,
Stings her mezzo voice in my skull
Croons and torments a brooding lull.
I can hear her singing to me,
Nocturne she lingers by decree
In the lachrymose chair I mull
Alone torments a brooding lull.

Tourniquet

Oh, Tourniquet where is your salvation?

Blood slithers from my latticinio veins [33]

Skin white bleeds into red consolation

I watch it drip; the sound of dry bloodstains

Reminisces of memories in chains,

Oh, the true love of Death's eternal kiss

Link by link, drop by drop; it remains

In the thoughts I cannot grievously dismiss.

---

[33] Latticinio – An opaque white glass used in threads to decorate clear Venetian glass. In this case, the speaker's fragile skin is like glass as the threads represent the body's cuts, scars, and veins.

Prophecy

Raven

Its croak I hear beckons,

Flies into the window affright

As I watch it die in my sight,

The quiet dread reckons.

Dark Lilac

Dark lilac falls upon her breast

Her blue eyes never let me rest,

The crisp air sways her short blonde hair

I hear her heartbeat and slow breath;

Shield her from the embrace of Death,

The dark-violet leaves wither bare

Numbness grips beneath her pale skin,

The memories flash what has been

My Luscinia muse I stare.

The Huldra

Huldra sings and wears a crown of flowers
Undergo, and through the forest pass the hours,
Love, and she promises to bestow with dowers
Deceive, and prepare to die by her powers,
Remain, and judge not her tail that towers
Abandon, and misfortune take a man who cowers.

Wiccan

She's a wiccan,

Incense flutters her house

In an altar room

My heart races to thicken

The love she has for me; I douse.

The tarot cards shown before me

Render my soul her foresight

Consults a covet

To a friend I esprit,

A love blooms bright.

Numb

Numb

Of lustful desire

Loving three women;

Blood-leech.

Mud-breech.

Amend

Never knew she was there,

She was always a friend

Now a lover

Wounds recover,

Never knew love; amend.

Gentleness

Roads with no end,

Truth of the calm river

Flows a forgotten way shiver

From the delicate light,

The stars, moon, earthen tones ascend

Her to a river white,

We both transcend.

Cartomancy

Love forms in various stages,

Continuum paces

Never stops the written pages,

Endless cycle chases

Fast-slow; in a constant motion

Phases through a strange emotion.

Love blooms patient graces

As vulnerability ages.

Susceptibilities are drawn

From time and seasons spent,

Let go what was already gone

The stepping-stone ascent

Leads to the light out the tunnel.

Take what is learned from each trunnel [34]

So new love will augment

---

[34] Trunnel – A wooden peg that is used to fasten timbers in shipbuilding; water causes the peg to swell and hold the timbers fast.

For a better beautiful swan.

An endless field of open green
Lies upon what could be,
All walls are broken; never seen
In the growth that is key.
Growth to battle against the storm
Self-growth in order to transform
New love from seed to tree,
The Lovers' tree of life serene.

As all-natural things will decay,
The Lovers' tree of life
Shall also too wither away,
Remember, time's keen knife
But do not despair from sorrow,
Lovers cherish ever' morrow.
Reversed tarot Death's strife
Harrows a loneliness to weigh.

$\mathfrak{Starr}$

The grandfather clock starts to speak,

Its charms and tolls harrows mystique

Oh, bell jar, my dearest Starr,

What glows meaning of your fluorspar?

Pretty shades of lavender hue

Its charms and tolls harrows mystique

Within my melancholy view,

Oh, my beautiful Starr's physique.

Elvira fuels my *ira*,[35]

With its tint of clear orange bitters

Its charms and tolls harrows mystique,

The pale stillness upon her cheek.

Among her gravestone I implore,

"It's your love I wish; nothing more,"

---

[35] Elvira as in reference to the alcoholic drink. Ira – Latin word for anger.

Dearest Starr, our love did bespeak

Its charms and tolls harrows mystique.

Guess Who?

Dare to guess who; this woman I adore?

Aglow her deep brown eyes revive me still,

Name written in the words who this is for,

Impatiently I wait for her until

Embellishment blooms her in natural thrill,

Love is patient, pure; she is worth the toil

Longing for her commitment; we'll

Endeavor to build a bond that can't uncoil.

My Parents

These days are now gone

But I must live on,

The lark withers in the dark

No longer singing,

No longer ringing,

Death grips my childhood's spark.

Black Rose

I am

A Romantic

Where romance is dying;

No more

The days

Of Passionate

Commitment now gone;

Faithless,

My hope

For a true love

To breathe a burning flame;

Sorrow

Grieves me

To a lonely

And hollow despair;

Forlorn.

Necrosis

Pendulum in my brain does shrive

Strange times to be alive,

Death and despair

Ensnare

Hollow

Walls; I wallow

Tormented by its call,

Forever, it swings me enthrall.

Unattainable

No spring can shimmer its water

Like she; I see, with her daughter,

Motherhood transforms her beauty in the light.

The sun shines behind her dark hair,

Her smile gaze most tender fair

My sweet friend, look what you created so bright.

How your dress in white falls among

The bedded leaves, your spirit young

Radiates in the purest form of love.

Fatherhood is what I desire

But broken romances mire,

When shall I ever know it; such love thereof?

Concupiscence [36]

Juniper radiates a tender glow,

Amble her eyes in a most luscious hue

Consumes her; shrouds her with a darken woe

Kindles a passion growing within view.

Imperious my heart; with its yearning

Empties and disdains my soul's countenance,

Careless, these flaming sentiments churning

Oppress action from my brain's discountenance.

Pale is her skin with its seductive lure

Embers the black tinge of her mascara

Love, ravage another I adjure

A fervor which paints an ephemera.

Never to fade, and never to pervade,

Demulcent your love, never to dissuade.

---

[36] Concupiscence – Strong sexual desire; lust.

Death Bed

When my heart is nothing but dust,

A memory;

A soul

Lost

Will you love me?

The bare

Frost

Within my mind

Numbs life's

Cost.

Acedia

I am born to die and die I must

For the dawn rises and the evening falls;

A state of listlessness or torpor, hopelessness

And vague unease; a slave from within broods

Despair, the master of all, fashions me chains

Enthrall its whisper ensnares, and ferries me Stygian

Across its gloaming call; look within the eigengrau

Where my soul is only a smidgeon.

Memories cherished and forgotten wallow

Like the seasons' cycle, and time intervenes,

Restlessness devours, not living, always shattering;

My umbra torments my Athene, enslaves any voca-

tion

I endear; somber, unfeeling weans the essence of my

being;

Charon reaps my melancholy demeanor with its tene-

brous,

"Another self-taken is one forsaken," bellows the fer-
ryman's bells
Where my soul is somatic in its psychological caligi-
nous.

His bells ring, ring, ring from the mere sleepiness,
sickness
And debility; a moral failing from my saturnine-beat-
ing heart
Longing for the self-love and affection of what was
once mine,
Depression ensures the anguish of any Aurora;
Cadaverous the screams which caterwaul
And scorch my ears along the crepuscular stream;
Death basks; it was, it is, and is always my only salva-
tion
To remedy against the sorrows of the false dream.

Illusive are the dreams of love, happiness, and pros-
perity

For their seductions string me a puppet of rotted de-

cay,

Lifeless, feeble, and broken these hopes of fancy;

Death is the only guarantee promised always there

Always ready with open arms

My soul is blackened and phototropic

Life…

It is bleak and misanthropic.

Enchantress

Gorgeous, her visage of black and white
Renders my heart eerie and strange,
Alluring dark poet write
Curious lore; derange.

Enchantments casted on me,
Inspired by her craft mundane
Flutters dreams; none beautiful as she.

Raven hair; pale skin radiates thee,
Her image seeps my forlorn brain
Thy hand weaves macabre esprit.

She is all but a dream,
Purely hopeful but futile
As I write my poem on this ream,
Cursed to never know her is brutal.

Fly Me to Her

I desire companionship,

Not out of bitter loneliness

But love in a relationship,

I'm haunted by its ghostliness

Will she fly me to her?

Disappointment fills the vast void

Wasting all that time vulnerable;

The openness once shined destroyed

By suitors invulnerable,

Will she fly me to her?

Burden of desire to be loved

Rips my sewn heart from its seam,

When shall I find a beloved?

I once had such a gentle gleam

Will she fly me to her?

Attic Dweller

I'll be thirty; alone in this attic

As it's my monastery fanatic,

My own space and a place of creation

Where solitude thrives in isolation,

All will be dead.

There will be nobody to share my bed

Only flights of fancy within my head;

Reading in the comfort of my own books

Writing literature and musical hooks,

I'll be thirty.

All will be dead, alone, nothing sturdy

To sustain any sustenance; nerdy

Inside my own world daydreaming of love

That will never happen; this room above

My chambered tomb.

Forever suffering eternal gloom,

I sense and fear my own impending doom.

I, an attic dweller, will die too soon

To know what it means to live the bright moon

Wains on its dread.

Murder of Crows

I ponder

Writing with a feeble mind,

Death surrounds me and keeps me morbidly blind,

The keys tap and click with every stroke,

As a bird does croak,

Rustled wings

Weary things

This corvid does foil;

It sits on the condenser coil

Outside as I glare through the windowpane

More of them flock gather in a binding chain

I maunder.

Lovers' Memento

Years gone since I made love to her

Embers within my mind

Tender;

Every breath, touch always does stir,

Nude in her blanket twined,

Splendor.

Jacqueline

Now grieving our love long and gone,

Knowing from a friend, you've moved on

With a swain lover,

I rediscover

And hover; Now withdrawn.

I wonder if I cross your mind

As ever, hoping we'd rebind,

Regret I do not

Our broken love brought

Lessons taught

Intertwined.

I learned self-love and self-care

And still cherish all we did share,

I always miss you

Desire us two to renew as a pair.

Penumbra

Profound

Night sky is dark,

I'm bound

Hidden,

Cloaked in darkness

Bidden;

New moon

Born, who am I

To swoon?

Mausoleum

The waxing crescent joyous and curious

Tends timid, conservative in nature,

Tendencies to cling my past injurious

Mausoleum wilts my heart's crenature,[37]

Wherein here lies, rests, my soul's comfort zone

Drained in energy; instinct does ensure

Security above written in stone,

Nocturnal light shines within this tomb's lure,

Its shadows reflect my darkened allure.

---

[37] Crenature – A shriveled red blood cell observed in a hyper-
tonic solution.

Loneliness

When friends gather round BC's Bar

All grows brighter over par

For we drink and cavort each star,

They shine, everyone, but I spar.

My half-shadow torments me

Amidst a boozy, deep sea,

I'm torn and high in drinking

To suppress normal thinking

There's no lover to foresee.

I heft this glass

Wallow alone

No lovely lass

A heart of stone.

Self-Perfection

An amazing mentor

And guide through others' storms

That same impulse transforms

Perfectionism.

Its compulsion renders

Tragically back to me

Like wax-gibbous fuzee[38]

Never perfect.

Nearing full potential

Predisposed as caring

Nurturing, calming

What of myself?

---

[38] Fuzze – A friction match with a large head that will stay alight in the wind. The speaker references perfectionism as this type of match and claims perfectionism will never stay "lit" because of the waxing gibbous phase.

Depression

Driven internal pain and strife

What's logical?

Illogical?

What wants my heart with love and life?

A multitude

Of desires brood,

Shatter me in different angles,

Lethargic death

Draw my last breath,

Full moon casts shadows and strangles.

Gibbous Death

I die

Whereby

The soul's petals

Tumble

Crumble

Wilt and settle.

Deeper

Reaper

Your reflection

Tender,

Render

Death's affection.

Evanescent Love

Tempted

By the Fates of Death,

All slows; frozen in time,

Holds onto the past out of love.

Solemn

Love looking back blinds the present,

Unhealthy rumination

Burdens the mind

Somber.

Coraline [39]

Friends of friends, married and engaged

Streams social media

Breeds isolation; acedia [40]

Angsts my heart as loveless and aged.

I'm a waning crescent loner,

Near darkness; love is like Hoenir [41]

Strong, beautiful, but dulled and caged.

Those single burdened by baggage

Broken shatters my soul

Too eccentric to relate as whole,

Too afraid to self-un-package

We are damaged and hold value;

Polished but feel a disvalue

"Not to die alone," our adage.

---

[39] Coraline refers to the name of the poetic form used here. It is a modified Italian Octave invented by the poet Lisa Morris.
[40] Acedia – Mental sloth; apathy.
[41] Norse mythology: one of the Aesir having a strong and beautiful body but a dull mind.

Paradise

An electric spark

Raptures me,

Norse pagan in dark

Esthete. [42]

Shimmers of crystal

Filigree

Wrapped like a pistil

Burns carefree.

"Goin' to Valhalla?"

Implores she,

Beautiful calla [43]

You would be.

---

[42] Esthete – One who professes great sensitivity to the beauty of art and nature.
[43] Calla – A South African plant widely cultivated for its showy pure white spathe and yellow spadix.

Lugubrious

Gloaming

Shadows

Whisper pathways,

Prey and cycle patterns;

Burdens accumulate

Tormented, wretched,

Weary.

Hel's Fire & Ice

Stoic fire embers what's left,
These icy veins
Congeal my heart and split a cleft
To what was once there light bereft
Remains and binds me in its chains,
A life without love is not,
Ice spreads, crystals internal pains
Soul is wrought,
Suicide reigns.

Awakening

Stop

My *dear*

Shieldmaiden

Can't you *see my*

Eyes gazing, staring

Tenderly *heart breaking*

Wishing it was me, not him

Embracing you, *not touching you,*

While you're hugging him not me

In your arms, *holding us?*

Your serenity

He knows, *I know*

But who has

Your *worth*

Love?

Thine Embrace

Thor's thunder roars my frame

To sunder gentle love

Its sentimental warmth

Glows forth; thy tender touch

Leaves a smutch on my soul.

As I lie in *Folkvang* [44]

Wherein Freya's beauty

Shines, hers cannot match thine.

---

[44] Folkvang – "People field." A meadow or field ruled over by the goddess Freya.

Alanna

All this heart desires is to love and be loved,

Longing for her, the one who enamors my soul

And sets ablaze all thought and emotion,

Never to see and hold again,

Never to see and hold again,

Any effort given, tried, no notion

Sustains, withstands; but creates a dark gaping hole

No communication, no shieldmaiden beloved.

Weeping Willow

I am

Beside

Bitterness,

Senseless

Wounds to grow

Weeping willow

Dark; rigid

Forever?

Tarot of Ashes

Deathless,

Lifeless cycle

Harrows gloaming sorrows,

My love of myself and others

Is rendered for Judgment,

What's not and is

My fate?

To die alone

Or to love yet again?

The Lovers' card is never there

Past, present and future,

Magician runes

Reversed,

The Queen of Swords

In its shadowed reading

Shows many burdens of the heart;

Emotions are astray,

Withered unto

Ashes

Pulverized bone

Fragments are what remains

Letting go of love that was real

Channels through shades of light

And of darkness to heal.

What is now left

After

Transformation

When I feel unworthy

Of such love and warm affection?

These phases are nothing

But lifeless and

Deathless.

Writer's Remorse

In darkness

I wallow alone

In a tomb

Where a truth here lies.

I type, write

Hopeful words

None dare to compose

Vulnerability.

What is all this worth?

Woeful words

Lamenting on paper

Mean nothing.

My voice in shadow

Lost in woe.

Compression

Buried alive,

Darkness devours

My body, thoughts deprive

Every inch of these walls,

Melancholy gloom

Thrives; death will shrive.

𝕮orvid & Friends [45]

Corvids in a line

Jabber and dine carrion

Hark, and clarion!

---

[45] Refers to the fellowship of the Curious Corvid Publishing community.

Abigail

What heart shambles in my own chest
Of her green eyes and tender gaze,
How her dress curve o'er her breast
Meets her smile and skin amaze;
Her dark black hair and shoulders rest
Where in her chamber she now lays.

Memories in sleep forever,
Her graceful voice croons in my head
Which swoons so lithe wheresoever,
Delicate her cheek rosy red;
What face so pale will not sever
How pure, and deep this love does thread.

And of that love, and o'er this veil,
I mourn, I weep, yet cherish,
Her figure so still, and lips so frail,
Only next to her will I perish,

A tomb at peace my Abigail,

Together make love our parish!

St. Joseph Byzantine Catholic Church

Hark, as the crows and ravens call the end,

The bells toll nigh, beyond the abbey's yard

Dig, dig, dig; the shovel's work shall descend

Thy grave and mine. To die alone, sweet bard

Thine corvids will feast on the bodies marred,

The gray sallow skies creep over yonder

Wherein the halls, thy soul and mine wander.

Remembrance

Death shall be my bride and mine only heir,

As I relate this grim and ghastly thing

Whilst I write, long gone to shadows elsewhere

Within the solitude of my wellspring,

Lost loves, lost selves, hath visited threadbare

Tormenting me, haunting me, they doth wring

My soul forever in gloaming sorrow,

Where I desire no more tomorrow.

Aloneness

Feeble

Is courtship,

Romance of two

Or more; nothing lasts

Who could love me,

My darkness

Alone.

Forsaken

I abandoned myself to death's embrace,

Five years hath gone; memories here written

In this mausoleum tome, ne'er efface

What was once mine to hold ago smitten,

Born a creature of dread was then bitten

By me to fill this insatiable void

I'll bleed myself dry with this stake piton

Hopefully it rots every single sinusoid. [46]

---

[46] Sinusoid – Tiny endothelium-lined passages for blood in the tissue of an organ.

Moonglade

My head rests upon the spot we once laid,

Here where winter's snow and bitterness

Bears only remnants of us here dismayed,

The moment we shared casts a brittleness

Time devoured, nothing lasts forever,

I stare where you were, flashbacks of your face;

I enjoyed what we had here together

Listen, what heart of mine had such a place

Coldness of the moon shines in the distance

The courtyard's water froze its softened tune

The moonlight gives warmth to my existence.

As my soul intertwines between death's blooms,

My eyes grow heavy and begin to close

Death, my love, is the blanket of all woes.

David Grinnell is a poet, author, and literary scholar from Cleveland, Ohio. He was born 1992 in Norfolk, Virginia, but grew up in the suburb of Bedford. In 2014 he attended Cleveland State University and graduated with his bachelors in English. Grinnell draws inspiration from vulnerability. He reflects and portrays love alongside hope, melancholy, and even occasional despair. Currently, he is finishing up his masters in English at Cleveland State University and emphasizes upon Romanticism and the Gothic. When he isn't writing, Grinnell is a local musician who performs as the solo artist Dave Grinnell and is in the band Naissance.

9 798986 300320